Jason
and the
Mischievous
Mongoose

Jason
and the
Mischievous
Mongoose

Nancy Sheppard

REGULAR BAPTIST PRESS
1300 North Meacham Road
Schaumburg, Illinois 60173–4888

Library of Congress Cataloging-in-Publication Data

Sheppard, Nancy D., 1960–
    Jason and the mischievous mongoose / Nancy D. Sheppard.
        p.   cm.
    Summary: Ten-year-old Jason, the son of a missionary in Liberia,
doubts the effectiveness of prayer when he loses his prized toy truck
and thinks he might lose his pet mongoose.   .
    ISBN 0–87227–172–2 (pbk.)
    [1. Mongooses—Fiction.   2. Liberia—Fiction.   3. Prayer—Fiction.
4. Missionaries—Fiction.   5. Christian life—Fiction.]   I. Title.
[Fic}—dc20   91–40480
                                                              CIP
                                                              AC

JASON AND THE MISCHIEVOUS MONGOOSE
© 1991
Regular Baptist Press
Schaumburg, Illinois

Printed in the United States of America.

To my own missionary kids,
John-Mark, Melodie and Nathan.

Contents

CHAPTER 1

A New Pet

J ASON STEWARD laughed. The little brown ball of fur raced toward him and jumped into his lap. With its pointed nose twitching, the animal searched Jason's pocket. Jason's cracker disappeared into its eager mouth. Golden crumbs bounced on its long whiskers.

"Oh, Pepper, you silly mongoose!" nine-year-old Jason said, laughing. He playfully tugged the animal's long tail. "You're just lucky we're missionaries here in Africa. Not many people would put up with you, right?" He rubbed his furry pet between the shoulders. Pepper looked up into Jason's blue eyes. He pawed with swift, tiny strokes. The small animal collapsed into the soft nest he had formed in Jason's red T-shirt.

Jason leaned back on the couch. He continued to rub

9

Pepper's shoulders. His free arm made a rest for his sweaty, blonde head. Jason looked sideways out the screened window. He watched a small brown lizard race up a tall mango tree. Its green branches shaded the house from the hot African sun. A speckled hen gathered her chicks under her wings for an afternoon rest. In the distance he saw the thick, green jungle.

The kitchen screen door slammed shut. Jason jumped in surprise. "Hi!" his eight-year-old sister, Melanie, said breathlessly. She threw her long brown braid behind her shoulders. "The mangoes at the top of the trees are ripe now! Want to get some?" Her eyes were bright with excitement. Mangoes, an orangish fruit about the size of apples, were delicious.

"Sure, but let me sit here a minute. Pepper is taking a nap."

Melanie looked down at the resting mongoose. She scratched her sweaty forehead. "May I hold him later? If you'll let me, tomorrow I'll play trucks and cars with you. We could pretend that one of the cars is a tractor. We could be visiting Grandpa and Grandma Brist's farm."

"OK, Melanie. But let's climb up those trees and get some mangoes now. Why don't you go over and get the Kwia kids. Pastor Kwia and Daddy got home from the evangelistic meetings yesterday. I think they should be home. They'll want some mangoes too." Jason leaned back to rest once more. It would take Melanie at least ten minutes to get his Liberian friend, Bowman, and Bowman's sister, Senaway.

Melanie dashed out of the house. A startled chicken squawked and fluttered away.

Jason looked down at his mongoose and smiled. He remembered the first day he had seen Pepper. He had been in the kitchen with his mother and father when a young Liberian boy came to the door. He was carrying a small wooden cage with a straw handle.

"Bock, bock" the boy said, announcing his arrival in the

typical Liberian way. "I have an animal for you to see."

"Hey, Mom, what animal is that? It's so little to have such a loud squeak!"

"I believe it's a mongoose, Jason. Perhaps the boy selling him can tell us more," Mrs. Steward said.

"Ah, Missy," the Liberian boy answered, "the mongoose is not like any other animal. The mongoose is very clever. He can even kill snake. If you buy him, you will be very satisfied. For one dollar and fifty cents the animal can be yours."

Jason looked at the scared animal in the tiny cage. "Where did you find him? Won't his mother be looking for him?" Jason asked.

The Liberian boy peered into the small cage. "The ma was killed last night by hunters. The baby was with her. The baby is too small to eat."

Jason swallowed hard. He did not like to think about mongoose soup.

"Dad, Mom, may I buy him?" Jason pleaded.

Mr. Steward looked at the mongoose and then at his wife. "Well, Dear, it's up to you."

Jason's mother paused a moment. "Jason," she said, "you may have the mongoose. But you must promise to keep him out of trouble. You are also responsible for his care. He's still a small baby; he'll need to be fed at night. We'll show you what to do. Then you will be on your own. Your little brother doesn't wake up in the night to be fed anymore. I don't want to start getting up with animals."

"Mom, I'll feed him at night, I promise!" Jason said.

Mr. Steward looked at the small animal. "I've heard that mongooses are a lot of fun. I've also heard that they can develop some very bad habits, like eating chicken eggs. Can you keep him out of trouble, Jason?"

"Oh, Dad, of course I'll keep him out of trouble," Jason eagerly agreed.

Jason's parents showed him how to feed his baby mongoose. They used an old eyedropper. The drops of milk spilled into its eager mouth and were swallowed immediately. Feed. Squeak. Feed. Squeak. This went on until the animal was satisfied. Then, with a full tummy, he began searching his new home.

"What are you going to call this little guy, Jason?" Mr. Steward asked. "He sure is lively. He's as full of life and spice as Liberian hot pepper!"

"Why, then, I think I'll call him Pepper. Don't you think he looks like a pepper?" His dad agreed. Jason was glad to have the problem of a name settled.

"Can he sleep with me?" Jason asked with hopeful eyes.

His mother looked up from her cooking quickly. "No way, young man. There's no telling where that animal has been."

"But where will he sleep?" Jason asked.

"Looks to me like Pepper is choosing his own bed," Dad replied, pointing.

Everyone looked at Pepper. He was carefully examining an old tennis shoe. He crawled over the edge, sniffing carefully. His tiny body disappeared into the front of the shoe. Appearing once more at the heel, Pepper curled up into a ball and fell asleep.

That was two months ago. Pepper could now sleep through the night. During the day he ate table scraps and canned fish. He was also starting to catch and eat small lizards. He would catch them when they scampered up the porch screens. Pepper was growing bigger and stronger every day.

Pepper was also really fun to play with or even just to watch. His favorite thing in the world was to play in the dirty clothes basket. He would jump in from the edge and then just roll and roll. He looked like he was swimming in dirty clothes.

Jason was petting his furry friend when he heard Melanie return with Bowman and Senaway. Setting Pepper down on the floor, Jason ran outside to meet them. A yard full of mango trees was waiting.

The Birthday Gift

H APPY BIRTHDAY to you," Jason's family sang to him. Two-year-old Nathan babbled along.

"Make a wish, and then blow out the candles," his mother said. Jason looked down at the ten flickering lights on the chocolate cake. He thought of the tractor he had seen at a toy store in America. It was just like the one on Grandpa and Grandma Brist's farm. Jason closed his eyes and took a deep breath. One big blow and the bright fire died.

"How does it feel to be ten, Son?" his father asked.

"Um, it feels about like being nine, I guess," Jason answered, shrugging his shoulders. His father laughed.

"Well, everyone, let's dig in," Mr. Steward said. "This cake looks super, Honey." Mr. Steward cut into the large chocolate birthday cake.

"First for the birthday boy!" he said, placing a large piece on Jason's plate.

Jason waited until everyone was served. "Can Pepper have some, Dad?" he asked.

Pepper heard his name and rushed to the table. Mr. Steward looked down. "What's on your whiskers, Pepper?" he asked.

Everyone looked at Pepper, who was running around in circles under the table. Mrs. Steward spoke first. "Oh, oh. It looks like Pepper has been into the garbage again. That's egg yoke on his face."

"Pepper," Jason scolded, "haven't we told you many times to stay out of the garbage can! You naughty mongoose!" Jason looked up at his father. "Can he have some cake anyway, Dad?"

"I guess so," Mr. Steward said slowly. "Your birthday comes only once a year. Why shouldn't Pepper get to celebrate too?"

Jason spooned the crumbs from the cake plate into Pepper's bowl. He placed it onto the floor. Pepper stood on the edge of the bowl, his pink tongue darting in and out. Too slow. Pepper climbed into the dish and gobbled the remaining crumbs.

"Someone is going to have to teach Pepper some manners!" Melanie said, laughing. "The pigs on Grandpa's farm eat nicer than he does!"

"You're not much better, Melanie," Jason said. "You've got a chocolate moustache!" Everyone laughed as Melanie hurriedly wiped her mouth with a napkin.

"Uh, let me see. I think I'll wash the dishes before you open your gifts," his mother said in a slow, teasing voice. Jason gave her a crooked grin. He wiped chocolate frosting from his chin.

"Mom, I know I'll die if I don't open them soon. I don't think I can wait another minute!"

The family gathered around Jason. He knelt on the

floor to open his gifts.

"Oh, great!" Jason exclaimed as he opened the gift from Grandpa and Grandma Steward. "It's a Chicago Bears T-shirt."

Pepper climbed over the new shirt and grabbed the wrapping paper. "Hey, you want this, Buddy?" Jason asked as he wadded the paper into a ball. He threw it toward an imaginary basketball hoop on the door. Pepper scurried after the paper, arriving at the door just before the paper landed. Grabbing it in his teeth, Pepper shook the paper ball back and forth.

"He's going to shake his brain out. I wonder what he's trying to do," Melanie exclaimed. She reached out to grab the paper from Pepper. Pepper looked her in the eyes. He gave the paper another shake and darted into the kitchen.

"What's he doing?" Jason asked.

"Maybe he wants to make a nest out of the paper. You know how he likes to be comfortable," Jason's mom answered.

Melanie spoke up. "I bet he's got a hiding place behind the refrigerator. I saw him come out of there yesterday."

"Can I open the next present, Mom?" Jason asked. He tore the paper off a package from Melanie and Nathan. "Thanks, guys. I can use these pencils for school."

The big red package was from his parents. He ripped the paper off it. "Oh, thank you, Dad and Mom! A soccer ball! Now I'll be able to play soccer with my friends." Jason tore the ball out of the box it came in. He tossed it to his father.

"I'm glad you like it, Son," Mr. Steward said, bouncing the ball off his toe. "Why don't you go ahead and open your last gift.

Jason looked at the tag on the remaining gift. Grandpa and Grandma Brist. I wonder if they could possibly know how much I want a tractor, he thought. Jason carefully pulled the tape up. He peeked under the paper at the box.

"Dad, it's a farm set!" Jason exclaimed as he ripped off

the paper and threw it to Pepper. "Look at the John Deere tractor!" Pepper raced between Jason's legs and out to the kitchen, dragging the red paper behind him.

"This is the most beautiful set of matchbox toys I've ever seen! It even has a carrying case. Oh, Dad, Mom, this is great! May I go and play with it in the sandpile?"

"Sure, you may go," said Mrs. Steward. "The sandpile is nice and big these days. The fresh sand for the cement blocks for the new church building just came in."

"Come on, Melanie! Let's go find Bowman. He'll want to play with it too. Mom, may I take a piece of cake to Bowman?"

"That would be fine, Honey. Better take one for Senaway too. Why don't you put your new things in your room. I'll cut some cake for your friends."

Jason grabbed the new shirt, pencils, ball and farm set. Tossing the carrying case onto the bed, he pulled open the top dresser drawer. His eye caught the picture hanging above the dresser. Neatly printed above the photo of a small boy praying beside his bed were the words "Prayer Changes Things." Jason smiled to himself as he read the words. It was nice to know that God cared about him and listened when he prayed.

"Hey, Mom!" Jason called from his room. "Have you seen my new shoelace? I need to fix this shoe, and now I can find only one shoelace."

Mrs. Steward answered from the kitchen. "I haven't seen it. Did you look by the toys? Maybe it got put in with them by accident."

Jason looked. Not there. Oh, well, I'll just be careful when I walk, he thought as he headed toward his mother.

"Hey! There it is!" Sure enough, a long black shoelace lay between the wall and the kerosene refrigerator. "Pepper, you're a thief!" Jason said as he grabbed the shoelace. His hand bumped a sticky eggshell. "Yuck!" he grunted.

"You're not going until you clean up the mess Pepper has made there, Jason," Mrs. Steward said. "It's not even safe to have that paper under there. It could catch fire."

Jason cleaned up Pepper's collection without complaint. The eggshell. Three crayons. A key. The wrapping paper.

The cake was ready to go. Jason and Melanie raced from the house to find Bowman and Senaway. Startled chickens scattered as the door slammed. Tall mango trees lined the path, and overripe peach-colored fruit smeared the bottom of their shoes. They could hear the chatter of African gray parrots overhead. The air smelled heavy with rain.

"I sure am glad that Dad is working with Pastor Kwia," Jason said. "It'd be awful if the pastor didn't have kids. The Kwias have someone for you and someone for me. Did I tell you that Bowman is teaching me to hunt with a slingshot? I'm not good at it like him."

"Is your slingshot the thing that looks like a big wooden wishbone with a huge rubber band attached?" Melanie asked.

"Yeah. Bowman made it for me."

"That sure was nice of him," Melanie said.

Jason and Melanie walked past the rows of mud block houses. They greeted passing women and children. Many of the women were carrying heavy loads of wood on their heads. A large black rooster crowed in front of the Kwias' house.

"Bock, Bock," Jason and Melanie said in unison.

Eleven-year-old Senaway came to the door. Her dark hair was braided in tiny rows. Baby Martha, tied onto Senaway's back with a bright cloth, was sleeping. A tiny black hand hung limply at her side.

"Good to see you, my friends," Senaway said, her large brown eyes shining.

"Good day. How are you doing?" Melanie asked.

Before Senaway could answer, Jason interrupted. "Is Bowman home?"

"The boy is in the house," she answered in Liberian

English. "I'll get him. You can wait there," she continued, pointing to a large palm tree. "When he is finished with his work, he will reach to you. We have been too busy today. My ma, she is very sick. I wish that I could play today, but I must make food."

"We're sorry to hear that your ma is sick, Senaway. Did she go to the clinic?" Jason asked.

"Yes. They say she got serious malaria," answered Senaway. "Tell your pa and ma so that they can pray for her."

Melanie's forehead creased with concern. "Yes. We'll all pray for her. We brought something special for you, Senaway. I hope you enjoy it." Melanie held out the piece of cake.

"Thank you plenty!" Senaway said, smiling again. She reached for the cake Melanie held out. "I will eat it later. I must get back to my ma now."

Leaning against the palm tree, Jason and Melanie waited for Bowman. The woman from the next house cooked rice over an outdoor fire. Her daughter sat on a small wooden stool, stripping feathers off a dead chicken. Dark, curly-haired children played at their mother's feet. Nearby, a red rooster stretched his neck and crowed noisily. A group of men sat on a small porch, talking loudly.

Five minutes later Bowman bounded out of the small mud-block house. "Oh, the way my sister can make me work!" the nine-year-old boy complained. "I don't like it when my ma is sick." Sweat clung to his dark forehead.

Jason was too excited to worry about Bowman's complaints. "Look! I just got a toy tractor for my birthday. My grandfather and grandmother sent it to me from America."

"Wow! The toy is too fine. We can play together, yes?" Bowman asked.

"Of course, that's why I'm here. Oh, I almost forgot. Here's some birthday cake for you. It's chocolate."

Bowman reached for the cake. "I've never had chocolate cake before. What is it like?"

"Well, try it and you'll see!" Jason said, laughing.

Bowman nibbled a corner of the cake. He rolled the chocolate crumbs around on his tongue. "Oh, this is too fine!" he exclaimed. Jason and Melanie watched as Bowman slowly ate, making each bite last as long as possible. His tongue snaked out of his mouth, licking the last of the frosting off his dark lips. "Heaven will be filled with chocolate cake, my friends!" he announced.

Jason and Melanie laughed. Grabbing ripe mangoes off the nearest tree, they headed toward the big sandpile.

CHAPTER 3

The Tractor

EVERY DAY, after finishing their chores at home, Jason, Melanie and Bowman played. They especially enjoyed the new farm equipment. Senaway could not play because she was caring for her mother. Often other children joined them. Using their hands, small shovels and sticks, the friends built roads and imaginary villages. Leaves became roofs for houses. Tin cans became huts. Small cardboard boxes became larger houses. The children carried water to fill their imaginary rivers and lakes.

Pepper often joined them. It was fun to watch him dig into the sand. His little paws moved so fast that the children could hardly see them. Everyone had to watch him closely so he wouldn't ruin something when no one was looking. Sometimes, without warning, he would dash away. As everyone watched, he would chase a startled lizard up a tree. It was not safe for a lizard to sunbathe near the sandpile anymore. It could become mongoose food!

"These toys are too fine," Bowman said, packing a small red car into the blue carrying case. "The one I can enjoy the most is the tractor. I wish it was for me."

"I really like it too. I think this is the best toy that I've ever had," Jason said, holding it up for a better look. The green paint gleamed in the bright sunlight.

"My dad told me that if I take good care of it, it will last for many years," Jason continued. "I try to remember to put it away when I'm done playing. Sometimes Pepper gets into the case and spreads the toys all over the house! He even knows how to lift the lid off. I have to lock it just right." Jason blew the sand off the tractor. He put it into the case and snapped the lid shut.

"Some of the boys want to play football tomorrow, Jason. Can we all play together and use your ball?" Bowman asked, standing up.

Jason laughed. "I wish the world would get together on this one. It seems funny that in America the same game you call football is called soccer. Anyway, that sounds fine with me. See you tomorrow."

Jason walked slowly toward home, swinging the case at his side. Pepper followed behind, squeaking loudly.

"Hey, guy, what's the problem? You want a ride?" Jason leaned over, and Pepper crawled up his shirt to his shoulder. "Hey, don't get sand in my face!"

Nearing his house, Jason saw his dad loading up the motorcycle. Mr. Steward tied a water jug to the plastic basket on the back of the big bike. Mrs. Steward stood by, holding a small bag of her husband's clothes.

"Hey, Dad! Where are you going?" Jason yelled, running across the yard.

"I'm going to Ziah. I'll be there overnight," Dad answered.

"Why are you going there?" Jason asked.

"They're having evangelistic meetings. Pastor Kwia asked me to help out tonight and tomorrow. Would you like to come?"

"Sure!" Jason answered. "Let me get some clean clothes. Mom, will you watch Pepper for me?"

"Yes, I'll take care of Pepper while you're away," Mrs. Steward said. "Don't forget your toothbrush!"

Jason hurried onto the porch. He threw his case of cars onto the small straw table. He leaned over, and Pepper jumped from his shoulder to the table.

"You'll be a good mongoose while I'm gone, won't you, buddy?" Jason asked. Pepper squeaked and wiggled his whiskers.

"Hey, Jason, can I play with your farm set while you're away?" Melanie asked.

Jason rushed past her to his bedroom. "Sure. But you have to stay in the house or on the porch. And you have to put everything away when you are done, OK?" Jason yelled from the back of the house as he grabbed a clean shirt.

Outside the motor roared. "Coming, Jason?" his dad called.

Jason slammed the drawer closed, rocking the "Prayer Changes Things" picture that hung above the dresser.

"Coming, Dad." Jason rushed past Pepper. Pepper was busy running in circles around the top of the straw clothes basket. "Bye, guy. Be good," he called to him. He gave his mom a quick kiss.

"Be good, everyone!" Mr. Steward shouted above the roar of the motorcycle. The two headed down the muddy trail to Ziah.

CHAPTER 4

Missing

H I, MOM," Jason yelled from his seat on the back of the motorcycle. His father turned off the engine. The big bike rolled to a stop, scattering two lazy chickens. His mom opened the door, and Pepper ran out to greet them.

"Hi there, little guy. It's good to see you." Jason rubbed his nose in Pepper's soft fur. Pepper's whiskers tickled Jason's nose.

"Did you have a good time, men?" Mrs. Steward asked. She gave Mr. Steward and Jason each a kiss.

"We sure did, Honey," Jason's father answered. "The meetings went really well. Pastor Kwia and I have decided that we will go back next week. Three people trusted the Lord as their Savior."

"That's great, Dear!" Mrs. Steward said.

Jason's father continued. "The Christians there are interested in getting a church started. Look what the people sent home with me."

"What a big stalk of bananas!" Jason's mom said. "Did Pastor Kwia get some?"

"Yes, they gave him a stalk the same size. They were grateful to us for coming. God is really blessing there," Mr. Steward said.

"How was Pepper while I was gone, Mom?" Jason asked, rubbing his mongoose behind its small ears.

"Well," Mrs. Steward answered slowly, "he was pretty good, I guess. I think that you ought to have a look on the porch."

Jason slid off the back of the motorcycle. He hurried to look through the porch screen. "Hey! Why are all my toys dumped onto the floor?"

"Well, this morning I had a ladies' meeting at the church. Before leaving, I went out to the porch to lock the door. I noticed then that your case had been dumped."

"Why didn't Melanie put them away? She promised me she would put them away!" Jason whined.

"Melanie was away this morning. I know she didn't play with them," Mrs. Steward answered.

"Then who did? Nathan?" Jason demanded.

"Nathan may have flipped the latch open, but it was Pepper that dumped them. When I brought Nathan in for breakfast, all the toys were in the case. When it was time to leave, I went out there to lock the door, and the toys were everywhere. I was in a hurry, so I just locked the door and left."

"Pepper, why do you have to be so messy?" Jason said. He held the furry animal to his face and gave him a kiss. "You should help me clean up, don't you think?" Pepper squeaked loudly, jumped down and ran behind a chair.

Picking up the toys took only a minute. Jason put each small vehicle into its proper compartment. "Hey! Where's the tractor?" Jason asked loudly to no one in particular.

"I'm sure it's there, Jason," his mother called from inside the house.

"I don't see it!" Jason cried.

"Why don't you look behind the refrigerator? Maybe Pepper took it."

Jason looked behind the refrigerator. He also looked everywhere else that he could think of. "Mom, I don't see it anywhere!"

Mrs. Steward looked around. "Maybe it's outside. You know that Pepper can push the front door open if it's unlocked."

"Come on, Pepper. Show me what you did with it," Jason said. He stepped into the bright sunlight. Pepper darted between his legs and out the open door.

Jason searched the area around the house. No tractor. He looked around the house again. No tractor.

"I hate to say it, Jason," his dad said, "but I suspect that the tractor is gone."

"Oh, Dad, how can it be gone! I wish that Nathan hadn't touched the case. I know that it was in there yesterday."

"Blaming your brother will not bring the tractor back, Jason," Mr. Steward said quietly. "Have you remembered to pray about this problem? Remember what it says above the picture in your room? Prayer really does change things, you know. Do you want me to pray with you?"

"Do you think God cares about my tractor, Dad?" Jason asked.

"Well, the Bible says that God loves us more than a father loves a son. I know I love you a lot. So, if I care about you and your lost tractor, God must care even more, right?"

"I guess you're right, Dad." They went into Jason's room and sat on the bed.

"Dear Heavenly Father," Mr. Steward prayed, "You know how much this tractor means to Jason. I pray that if it is Your will, this toy will be found. In Jesus' name I pray. Amen."

"Thanks, Dad. I feel better now. I know that God will answer your prayer," Jason said.

"Why don't you take a break from your searching," Mr. Steward suggested. "Go do something with Bowman or one of the other boys."

"OK, Dad. I guess I will." Jason left the house. He shuffled down the path to Bowman's house. A parrot screamed above his head.

Jason neared the Kwias' house. He saw Senaway sitting under the thatched roof of the outdoor kitchen. Steam from a large pot of rice rose in front of her. Bright orange flames licked the bottom of the large iron pot. Senaway looked hot and tired.

"Hello, Senaway. How are you?" he asked.

"I'm OK, but my ma is still too sick," she answered, looking discouraged.

"I'm sorry to hear that. Our family has been praying for her."

"Thank you for your prayers. Are you looking for Bowman?" Senaway asked.

"Yes, is he here?"

"He's in the house. The boy will be no fun to play with today. His face is too long. I don't know why he is so unhappy," Senaway said.

"Bock, bock," Jason said loudly, facing the open door. After a long wait, Bowman appeared.

"What do you want?" Bowman muttered. His face was twisted into a scowl.

"I am too sad today, my friend. I went with my pa to Ziah last night. When I returned today, my tractor was missing," Jason said.

"Oh," was all Bowman said. His lower lip stuck out.

"So, you want to play ball? Maybe I will feel better if I think of something other than the tractor," Jason said.

"Um, no. I don't feel like playing ball."

"We could play with the other farm toys in the sand. You want to do that?" Jason asked.

"No, no. I don't think I want to play today," Bowman said.

Jason looked at his friend in surprise. "But, Bowman, you always want to play. Are you feeling sick?"

"Uh, uh, yes. Yes, I think I'm getting sick. I'm going into the house to lie down. Good-bye." Bowman turned and went into the house, slamming the door behind him.

"See what I mean, Jason," Senaway said. "He's being strange today."

CHAPTER 5

Problems

JASON KEPT looking for the tractor. However, after three weeks of searching, it seemed hopeless. Besides, he had other problems to worry about.

Bowman had been coming over to hunt lizards. That was fine, of course. Unfortunately, his aim with a slingshot was much better than his mood.

"What's the matter, Bowman? Are you mad at me?" Jason asked for the third time. He threw Bowman's latest victim to Pepper. Pepper attacked the small dead reptile eagerly.

"Why don't you quit talking and start hunting?" Bowman snapped.

Jason shrugged his shoulders. "Show me how you do that again. I'm no good at this."

Bowman looked impatient. He explained, once again, how to aim and fire. Choosing the smoothest stones, he guided Jason's hands. Jason aimed, and the rubber band shot the stone toward a lizard. Miss.

Bowman aimed and fired. Hit.

Jason aimed and fired at another lizard. This one was sleeping. Jason still missed.

Bowman aimed at the startled, running lizard. Hit!

"I'm tired of this, Bowman," Jason said crossly. "Let's quit."

"I'm not finished yet. I want to get some more lizards for our chickens."

"Come on, let's do something else." Jason kicked the grass at his feet.

"No, I want to do more hunting," Bowman said. He searched the jungle for more lizards.

"Then I'm leaving!" Jason whirled away. Getting home, he stormed into the house, slamming the door behind him.

Melanie looked up from her coloring. "What's your problem, Sourpuss," she asked, taking out a red crayon.

"I don't have a problem, Bowman does. He brags." Jason's nose and eyes crinkled into a scowl.

"What did he say?" Melanie asked.

"Oh, he just thinks he's such a great hunter."

"Did he say that?"

"No, but I just know he thinks he's great and I'm stupid," Jason said. "Besides, it's none of your business."

Melanie smirked. "I think you have the problem, not Bowman. You're jealous."

"I am not! Take that back! You think you're so smart!" Jason stormed past Melanie to his room. "By the way, your picture looks stupid!" He slammed the door, shaking the back half of the house.

This is awful, Jason thought. What more could go wrong? Besides the problem with Bowman, he also had trouble with Pepper. Pepper was growing big really fast. He was getting into trouble. The family was forever finding things that he had stolen. Usually they were behind the refrigerator or in the dirty clothes basket. Sometimes it took several days for someone to find them.

That evening Jason found out that things could get worse. Jason looked up as his father came in from checking on the chickens. "Son, I didn't mention it the first time, but I feel that I must now. Our chickens have been doing just fine until recently. Tonight I found another chicken egg broken. This is the second. You know mongooses are famous for loving eggs. Where was Pepper this afternoon?"

Jason looked at the floor tiles. "I don't know," he mumbled.

"Don't forget the promise you made to your mother. You promised her you would keep Pepper out of trouble."

Jason had looked down at the floor, his eyes stinging. "Don't you think that Pepper is more important than a couple of chicken eggs?" he asked angrily.

"Remember, Jason," his father continued, "we count on those chickens for meat and for eggs. We can't have anything destroying them. Besides, if Pepper would steal from us, he would also steal from our neighbors. The Liberians depend on their eggs even more than we do. If the eggs don't hatch, many will have no meat at all. And, of course, the boiled eggs are really good for them too."

"What am I supposed to do, Dad?" Jason blinked to keep the tears from overflowing his eyes.

"Keep a closer eye on him, Jason. We can't keep an animal that steals eggs. And, Son, don't you think you should have a talk with Bowman about the way you acted this afternoon?"

How did he find out about that? Jason thought. Melanie and her big mouth! I don't have to talk to Bowman about today. I'm not the one with the problem.

CHAPTER 6

Eggs, Eggs, Eggs

J ASON WENT over to Bowman's house the next day hoping that Bowman would have forgotten yesterday's problems. For half an hour the two walked along the edge of the jungle with their slingshots. Jason talked about football, school and all kinds of things. Bowman just listened.

Finally Jason brought up what he had been thinking about the most.

"I don't know what I can do. I can't watch Pepper every minute! But I know that this stealing can't go on. My dad said that we can't keep an animal that steals eggs."

Bowman kicked at a stone with his foot. He didn't look at Jason. He picked up a smooth stone and placed it in his slingshot. Bowman looked at the large orange tree in front of him. Squinting into the sun, Bowman lifted his slingshot. Ready! Aim! Fire! A small green orange tumbled to the ground.

Jason picked up a stone and also aimed at an orange. Fire! A green leaf floated slowly to the ground.

"Oh, well. At least I hit the tree!" Jason laughed at his bad aim. He looked at the silent Bowman. "Hey, are you sick or something? Why aren't you talking?" Jason asked, touching his arm.

Bowman jerked his arm away from Jason's touch. "Do I have to talk all the time? The way that you can vex me! I don't want to be your friend again. I'm going home!"

"Hey! Don't be mad at me, Bowman!" Jason yelled after Bowman. But it didn't do any good. Bowman ran down the path angrily, looking like the sky before a tropical storm.

For several days no eggs were broken. Jason began to think that perhaps his problem with Pepper was solved. He hoped Pepper would forget about eggs. Maybe he would be satisfied with his fish and milk again.

"Hey, Jason. Isn't that Bowman coming down the path?" his mom asked. It had been a week since Bowman had run away in anger.

Before Bowman could say, "Bock, bock," Jason ran out of the house. Pepper darted out from behind the refrigerator and through the opened door. "Hey, it is good to see you my friend! You come to play?" Jason asked.

"I come to hunt," Bowman said, looking at his feet. "If I stay at the house, my sister will find work for me."

"Good. Let me get my slingshot!"

Jason and Bowman walked silently along the edge of the jungle looking for lizards. Neither talked about their argument.

"I have good news," Jason said, breaking the silence. "I've been praying that God would stop Pepper from eating more eggs. Since I've been praying, he hasn't eaten any more eggs. I'm really happy about that. I was afraid that my ma and pa would make me put him in the jungle."

Bowman ignored the conversation. "Hey, there's a big one!" Bowman said, pointing to a lizard scampering up a tree. "You try for this one. Here, this stone is a good one."

Jason shot and missed. Bowman aimed. The stone hurled through the air. Hit.

The loud roar of the motorcycle interrupted the hunters. "Hi, Dad! What are you doing?" Jason yelled. Mr. Steward brought the motorcycle to a stop beside the two boys.

"I'm just checking up on two of my favorite boys! How is the hunting going?"

"Not too well, Dad. I'm not a very good shot," Jason admitted.

"Well, I guess there are more important things in life," his dad said with a smile. "And how are you today, Bowman? How is your mother?"

"I'm OK, but my ma is not better. She's still in bed."

Mr. Steward looked concerned. "We will continue to pray for her, Bowman. Has she been to the clinic lately?"

"No, the money is finished. Medicine can cost plenty," Bowman answered.

"Well, guys, I had better go now. Have fun hunting." The motorcycle roared down the muddy path.

Jason was busy playing with Bowman. He paid no attention to what Pepper was doing. That night when his father came into the house, he had a concerned look on his face. He asked Jason to come outside with him.

"Jason," he said, pointing to a chicken nest, "we've got a serious problem. Another egg is broken." Jason looked at the nest. Crumbled shell and gooey yolk covered the remaining eggs. "Where was Pepper today?"

"I don't know. I was busy playing with Bowman. I wasn't watching Pepper."

"Son, if this happens one more time, that mongoose will have to go. We've talked about how serious this is. Do you understand, Jason?"

Jason's eyes filled with tears. Pepper, going? This

couldn't happen! "Oh, Dad, I promise I'll be really, really careful from now on."

"Son, I know how much Pepper means to you. I'm not trying to give you a hard time. But you know the rule about animals that steal eggs."

The lump in Jason's throat made it impossible for him to answer. He felt like he had swallowed an orange—whole.

CHAPTER 7

No More Chances

J ASON DID nothing during the next few days without Pepper in his sight. His dad was away preaching in a village. Jason did not want to greet him with bad news.

Every afternoon he checked the chicken's nests. Then he would play in the sandpile with Bowman or some of his other friends. Jason was tired of always missing the lizards while hunting. Playing with the farm equipment was more fun, even without the tractor.

"I really miss the tractor a lot. I sure wonder what happened to it," Jason said. Bowman made a road in the wet sand with his finger. "I was sure that it would turn up one day."

Bowman didn't answer. He turned his back to Jason and arranged several small sticks to make a bridge.

The soft hum of a motorcycle in the distance inter-rupted Jason's thoughts. "Hey! It's my dad! Come on, let's go to the house!" The boys grabbed the toys and stuffed them into the case.

They arrived at the house just as Mr. Steward's motor-cycle rolled up to the door. "Hi, boys! How have you been?" He grabbed Jason and squeezed him. With his free arm he reached out and tickled Bowman on the side. Bowman doubled over, laughing.

Mr. Steward got off the motorcycle. "I'm going to take a bath, guys," he said. "I feel like I brought that village home with me. I'm so muddy! Hey, get off of here!" Mr. Steward flung his arm at the rooster that jumped onto the motor-cycle seat. "Hmm. These chickens think they own the place," he muttered.

"Bowman, I want to be with my dad. Do you mind if we don't play any more today?" Jason asked.

"Oh, that's OK. I . . ." Bowman continued, but that was all Jason heard as he hurried into the house.

After his dad finished his bath, the family had an early supper. "Eggplant soup on rice! My favorite!" Jason said. "I think this is my favorite Liberian food. I especially like it made with chicken." Jason took a large spoonful of rice and heaped the soup on it. "This soup looks almost like chow mein, doesn't it? I wonder why the Liberians call this soup."

"I don't know, Jason," Mr. Steward answered. "I won-der what Americans would think if someone put Liberian hot pepper on their chow mein. I think Pepper wants some too, Jason."

Jason looked down at Pepper. He was running around the legs under the table, squeaking. "OK, Pepper, I'm coming. You'd better quit your begging! Mom's going to stick you out on the porch with nothing." Jason heaped rice and soup into Pepper's bowl. He carried it to the porch. Pepper ran eagerly in front of him.

"Help your mom clear the dishes, kids," Mr. Steward

said later, stepping out the kitchen door. "I'm going to check on the chickens."

Several minutes later he returned. From the look on his face, Jason knew it was bad news.

"Jason," Mr. Steward said, "there are two eggs broken in one of the nests. I'm sorry, but you know the rule. The mongoose is going to have to go back into the jungle."

Jason looked at his father and then at his mother. His mother looked like she was going to cry.

CHAPTER 8

The Picture

C RYING FELT good for awhile. Lying on his bed, Jason angrily punched his pillow. When no more tears would come, he stared at the ceiling and walls. He looked at the picture above the dresser.

"Huh! 'Prayer Changes Things.' I doubt it," Jason mumbled. "I hate that picture. If God cared about me, I'd have my tractor and my mongoose. Now I won't have either."

Jason jumped off the bed. He grabbed the picture off the wall and looked at it a moment. Flipping the picture upside down, he fiercely jammed it into the bottom dresser drawer.

"Jason," his mother said, knocking softly on the door.

"What?" Jason grunted, jumping back onto the bed. He stuffed his face into the pillow.

"May I come in?" Mrs. Steward asked through the

closed door. Jason didn't answer. After a brief pause, his mom opened the door and peeked inside.

"Are you OK, Honey?" she asked.

Jason didn't answer. The bed sagged a bit as his mother sat down on the edge.

"Jason, why don't you come out of your room now?" she asked, rubbing his back. "You need to take a bath anyway."

Jason felt his mother's warm fingers on his back. He sniffled a bit, then turned his face to the side. "I don't feel like getting up. I wish I could lie here until I die."

"Jason, I understand that this is difficult for you." She paused as if she were trying to think of what to say. "Do you want to talk about the picture? I notice that it's not on the wall."

Jason leaned up on his elbows. He studied the filling that balled up inside the pillow. "What's there to talk about? I didn't like it up there. It's babyish anyway. That boy in the picture was probably only three years old. I don't want a picture of a three-year-old in my room."

"Honey, you've never said anything about that before. Are you sure that's what the problem is?" his mother replied softly.

"I don't believe it anyway!" Jason snapped. He threw the pillow down.

"Don't believe what?"

"I don't believe that prayer changes things, that's what!" Jason said. "I'm going outside for a little while. Is that OK?"

Without waiting for an answer, Jason ran out of the room.

CHAPTER 9

Good-bye, Little Friend

JASON PUNCHED holes into the box for air and laid in soft grass for bedding. The box was ready for the long trip.

"Better say good-bye to Pepper, Jason. I'll be leaving in a minute," Mr. Steward said. He put his hand on Jason's shoulder. Jason shrugged it off angrily.

Tears poured into Pepper's fur. Pepper looked up into Jason's red eyes. He looked confused. His whiskers tickled Jason's nose.

"I'm going to miss you so much, little friend," Jason whispered. "Promise me that you will be OK. I love you, Pepper."

"Jason," Mr. Steward said softly, "I need to talk to Pastor Kwia. I want to ask him where I should drop off Pepper. He knows the jungle much better than I do. You may ride with me to his house and then walk home."

Jason placed Pepper onto his shoulder. He climbed onto the back of the motorcycle, being careful not to touch his father. The three rode in silence.

"It looks like Pastor Kwia was coming over to our house. There he is now," Jason's dad said. He turned off the engine and rolled the motorcycle to a stop.

"Hello, Teacher," Pastor Kwia said, laughing. "I was just reaching to your house. Instead, you come to me. I have good news. My wife, she is coming on fine now. The sickness has left her body."

"Praise God!" Mr. Steward said, resting his arm on Pastor Kwia's back. "He has answered our prayers."

Jason nuzzled his face into Pepper's soft fur. I wish He had answered my prayers, he thought bitterly.

"I wish our news was as happy as yours, Pastor," Mr. Steward said as he walked the motorcycle toward the Kwias' house. "Jason's mongoose is breaking eggs. We feel that we must return him to the jungle. Could you help us find a good place for him?"

"Oh, that is too sorrowful," Pastor Kwia said, turning to Jason. "I know that you must be feeling bad." Jason stuffed his face in Pepper's fur and did not answer. "Yes, I can help," he said to Mr. Steward.

"It's not right to keep him if he steals," Jason's father said, passing by the side window. He rolled the motorcycle to a stop in front of the house.

"I agree," Pastor Kwia said. "The stealing may be small now, but it will probably get worse. We must get rid of him."

The front door burst open. Bowman jumped down the stair, terror written all over his face. A streak of green flew through the air.

Pastor Kwia, Mr. Steward and Jason stared at the ground, not understanding. There lay the small tractor, brilliant green in the sunlight. They looked up at Bowman.

"Please don't get rid of me, I beg you! I won't do it again! I didn't mean to keep it. I took it when Jason went with his pa to Ziah. It was outside the door, just lying there. I was going to give it back, but I couldn't. And my ma needed the eggs to help her get better. I was going to—"

"Bowman, stop!" Pastor Kwia demanded. "What are you talking about!"

"Please don't get rid of me! I promise I won't steal again," Bowman begged, falling to his knees.

"Bowman, of course we won't get rid of you! What are you talking about?" Pastor Kwia demanded.

"But weren't you talking about me just now?" he asked.

The two men looked confused. A look of understanding crossed Jason's face. "Bowman," Jason said, "our fathers were talking about getting rid of Pepper, not you. I've told you before that my father would make me get rid of Pepper if he kept breaking eggs."

"I didn't think that he was serious. I broke the eggs. I broke one egg from each nest, and then took one of the good ones. I figured that your father would not count the eggs and that he would notice only the broken one. I knew he would blame Pepper. I'm sorry, Jason."

Pastor Kwia interrupted. "Bowman, how could you do such a thing!"

"Pa," Bowman said, tears running down his face like a river, "I thought that ma would die. She told me there was no money for medicine. The nurse at the clinic told her to eat eggs. I wanted to help."

"Son," Pastor Kwia said, "why didn't you talk to me about this? Mr. Steward helped us to pay the clinic bill and buy the medicine. How could you steal? We've taught you that stealing is never the answer to a problem."

"I'm sorry, Father. I'm very sorry," Bowman said. He turned to Jason. "Will you forgive me, Jason? I'll understand if you never talk to me again. I have been so bad."

"I forgive you for stealing." Jason looked at the ground, kicking the tufts of grass at his feet. "Will you forgive me for being jealous? I've been angry because you can hunt better than me. I'm sorry for that," Jason said.

"Of course, I forgive you!" Bowman said, grabbing Jason's shoulder. The boys hugged. When they pulled apart, they were both smiling.

"Son," Pastor Kwia said, "let's go into the house. I think we need to talk to the Lord about this, don't you?" Bowman nodded, and the two disappeared into the house.

"Jason," Mr. Steward said, putting his hand on Jason's arm. "I should apologize too. It was wrong of me to accuse Pepper without real proof. Will you forgive me?"

Jason threw himself into his father's arms, being careful not to squash Pepper. "Of course, I forgive you." Jason's tears made his father's shirt wet. Neither of them cared about that a bit.

Pulling away at last, Jason rubbed Pepper behind the ears. "Let's go home, Dad. I want to give Pepper a special treat."

Besides, he thought, I have a picture I need to hang back up!